The
Creep People

by

J. J. Williams

This book is entirely fiction.
Front and rear covers by JJ Williams.
This first edition published 2022.

Williams J. J.
The Creep People

ISBN: 9798418735225

THE CREEP PEOPLE

CONTENTS

PREVIOUSLY ON THIRD STREET

Tick tock:
Dead leaves fall from the clock
Of time,
While the trees wither in the wind
Of their blindness.
For old time's sake, woman,
Kiss me
And be done with your hard-boiled
Ways.
Time is now.
And time will be the end
Of me and you.

FRIENDLESS

I looked at the sun,
The sun looked away,
Then all of the world
Froze to death that day.

WITHERING WHEELS

He came running down the street
All naked and screaming
With all of his
Hopes and dreams ablaze
In his mercy-begging hands.
But the world had long lost
The trumpet of care and love,
And so, sadly,
He burned all up
Into the greedy hands of death
With debts waiting everywhere
For his coming children.

BUYING A FRESH HOUSE

I bought her mortgage
With a passion kiss,
I held her interest down!
I put curtains up around her legs,
And there I turned into a clown!
I turned her attic into a mind extension with
Cannabis grows good in warmth and power light!
I built her kitchen into her womb!
Yet now all is turning dark and gloomy -
Oh, I fear she will leave me very soon!
Trumpets out and search for armies
To blast out my love for her!
And let her hear those missiles explode
As I kiss her lightly upon her funky rear!
Love is back and dances akimbo
In the naked bedroom full of jazz tonight;
For now she is my house,
Of that I now prance with princely
Delight.

STIFF CHEESE

When her pants fell down
I kissed her.
When my pants fell down
She screamed!
Oh, the way of the worm
As weeds grow like women
In pastures rarely cleaned.

And so to the tower of
Spank Me Do
She has sent me -
There to waste away
In the swamp fields of despair!
A rare zombie crawls out of my brain
And turns me into a coffin
And flying,
Like a Bonaparte sigh,
I race gladly
To be free of her and her temper
Into the dead world of
Forever nowhere Jesus.

EMBER

The face of Ember glowing
And chiming like bells
From a broken city of funerals
All rushed and over-planned
By people who don't really care.

The face of Ember climbed to the very top
Of hope
Yet there only found desolation.

The face of Ember grew new limbs
And purpose
And there began to build his own world
Without the wet trousers
Of dreams and false hopes
That are driven into you at school
Like nails.

Did Jesus really cry for you?

The face of Ember
Lived long and plenty
With a field of kids to spare:
A poor wife drowned in child birth
With no glitter in her hair.

The face of Ember
Wept bitterly
When the wife rolled out to die.

The face of Ember
Begged no pity
As her spirit ran off up into the sky!

The face of Ember lived on
Like an empty mountain -
His blaze all dead and gone
And now he too into death romances
Just as the window cleaner
Begins to sing a new song.

THE BENDY WAY

A vampire has appeared on the street
On the doorstep of the night into day.
The people like onions are screaming
With tears to hopefully drive this beast away.

The vampire has started singing
His love of the church doom bell
That now roars out into the darkness
Of every mind that believes in a heaven and hell.

Now a garlic man has appeared to save us
And toward the vampire his steps resound
The puffy vampire sees him and screams
And there disappears without a sound.

So saved we all meander
And thank the garlic man with beer and cheer,
But the garlic man turns into a werewolf
And eats us all up from big toe to ear!

The world of human now runs away
And there they crash into a star
Where a new history awakes
As the star turns into a car!

The car drives away with power
And floats down to land on a new place
And the new place is called Planet Earth
Where total madness by the humans is given full
Birth and grace.

A CUCKOO

A cuckoo in the morning
Painting a moustache in the day
Then flying off to Venus
Where aliens build pyramids out of hay.

A cuckoo in the evening
Full of tea and wine
And he flies off to Beard World
Where ladies wear skirts made out of pink divine.

A cuckoo in the bedroom
Just as sex came out to play
Now the butcher's smashing bacon
And the police lock everyone away.

AN OLD TURN

Old man like a cigarette
Is burning away,
His packet now empty -
Yet with so much to say!

Hear the old girl
Like a church driven bell
Clanging and banging
The new world down to hell.

Nobody bothers
To listen, but say:
"Go pick up your ashtray,
And be off far away!"

In time
We all melt away.
Have no fear;
We're all going to die.

DUFF DO

Take the ship across the ocean -
Boom, boom, boom!

Sail the ship far away.

Find a place where freedom grows
Just like a fresh tree everyday.

Keep away your man-made religions;
We don't need gods to harvest our way.
Trumpets loud
Her sex has won me.
Sweet saxophone
My hands and kiss to play!

And the robot of life walks on.
We triumph in our own way.
Keep your scum beliefs to yourself;
In your own mind,
In your own hell.
For
What right have you to impose on others?

LETTERS WITHOUT PEOPLE

He came Dandy out of a cave singing
With naked humans in his head -
Yes, possessed by a sex demon
All bloody rude and sickly dread.
And now to persecute him
Like a mountain on a hill
A place where no flower could blossom
To embrace the good of summer's spill.
And so in harrow gloom he prospered
Masturbating everyday
Until the moment his body exploded
And all trace of him was blown away.
Now the sex demon has run off laughing
Into the nearest goodly town
Where tonight he captures a woman
And there in his lust she will
Surely drown!
But no – hark the envelope
Passing quaintly in the sky
Has seen the outrage below him
And now demands that the sex demon
By his hand will die!
And the sex demon sees him coming
And roars out a flame of war
But quick thinking the envelope throws out a sea wave
And puts out the sex demon
Forevermore.
Drowned in death the sex demon
Is washed away

And the woman and the town
Built a statue to honour the great envelope
Every life long day.

RED FACE

"Red Face!"
You say
Up high on a hill
The land of truth destroyed
By an invading evil will

Promises broken
All written down in blood
The end of a nation
Man did what he never should

All the wild beasts gone
Slaughtered in the sun
To starve to death the children
Now monster time has begun

"No help! No help!"
Sing it to the stars
As the evil carves up your history
With train, gun and cars

Still a ghost is waiting
The judgement bell in tears
Will man ever learn
To make good after all of these frightened years?

BEFORE WE WERE BORN

Paedophiles all over the streets
Wanking in the gloom,
While all the children play safe at home
Not coming out real soon.
Still.....
Some people drink more beer,
Some people drop down dead,
Some people wind up clocks
Just as you jump right out of bed.
"Where's the day gone?"
You say.
"Up your ass to heaven!"
I reply.
"I need a life,"
You declare.
Yet you never seem to try.
You can't just expect everything to be
Done for you.
You can't expect any favours in this life!
Yet still you dream;
As I do,
As we all do,
Even before we're born.

DONE WITH LOVE

I want to drink your pussy
Instead of this hairy beer.
I want to fuck you all night long
Instead of blowing smoke rings
In your ear.
But you're crazy for the beer -
You live it night and day!
While romance heads, like me,
Like the rest of the trash,
Get swept up and cast away!

So I'll beg the left hand again tonight
As I walk away deep into the
Dark and cold womb of the life.

JANE AGAIN!

Jane, Jane!
You have ravaged my life
And driven all of the horses away
Onto a sinking ship
From which they will never return
To me and play.
You wanted me completely -
All for yourself!
But when you finally got me
You put me to death.
Now with merry whistling
You disappear;
Leaving me naked
With my gravestone
Many years too near.

DEATH DANCE STILL

Her Earthly bottom pouted in the riches of sex.
I screamed for her body,
But my bells of desire clanged silently
Into the bowels of nothing
Where rats wait to drink the blood
Of every foolish man -
And so they should!
We, the fools,
Can never deliver the kiss of truth.
We should all be lined up against an angry wall
And shot to the dead
Without the saxophone of summer
Ringing joyously in our hairy ears.
Yet still they build roads
For no one to travel on!
A waste of everything -
A waste of all!
Now let me ponder
Life.

OLD MAN no 44

Old man you never quit
You're always there to play;
You've drained all of the vampires
Who drown the good out of the day.
The people look to government,
But you have more the wise;
You never forgot those politicians
Who once sent you off to fight and nearly die.
Old wounds are hard,
Yet old wounds are true;
They hold the key to revelation
Of the secrets that you once never knew.
Now grow your branches
And step out wide
Because
Old man we love you – yes,
You are our hope and pride.

LOVE POEM LOST IN TRANSLATION

Kiss-a my ass, bitch!

PINK HAZE AND LAUGHING

I stuck the needle in my arm
And screamed!
The empty room stood up
And took notice.

I felt the drug invade my body
And screamed again!
The bedsit door came crashing in
And in raced a flustered and confused
Do-gooding neighbour
Who could not comprehend what he saw
And fainted on the spot.
I embraced his body,
Stole the dots out of his eyes
And ate them into the vineyard
That was and is my body -
My temple of
Doom!

I pulled the rusting needle out of my arm
And henceforth rammed it up
The fainted neighbour's rectum -
That'll teach him,
The interfering git!
It's so nice to be cruel
When you only have drugs to live for.

I flashed into my pink knickers,
Then ran out onto the sex streets
To whore for cash.

The drug is always hungry.
THE DRUG MAKES ME DO IT!
"Feeed mee! Feeeeedd meeee!"
Ever on and on.
I swirl in a pool of dark and ANGRY madness!
"Argh!" I scream.
Nobody stops.
Nobody listens.
The people just fade away into the day
Like ghosts.
But now I'm floating -
I'm sailing away
In the arms of the drug
As it reinvents my day!
I smell the sea close at hand
And race over to the beach to dance
In the filthy sand,
And there I find myself
Drowning and drowning
In the merciless arms of the mighty waves!
How?
Why?
Die!

THE COW WHO CAME TO FEED

She's shit in the bath again!
Damn the dirty cow!
I should have left her
In the field where I found her.
She has been nothing but trouble
To me ever since
I brought her back here.
I must have been mad!
Grab a record,
Play some Jazz,
Chill out,
And hope she'll just leave.
But no!
A year later and she's
Still fucking well here!
She's using me
And tuning me into dead weeds!
I shall kill her – yes!
The knife takes my hand
And leads me into
My bedroom
Where she sleeps in
My bed;
Dreaming
My dreams
On
My pillows -
How dare she!?!

I slit her throat
And a sea of milk
Pours out of her udders.
Her beady eyes open to regard me,
Then they fall black
And sightless
And dead.
I have murdered her.
Now I shall eat her.
"Moooo!"

THE FORTUNATE SPARROW

What's up little sparrow?
Do your wings hurt tonight
As you shiver in the trees
In a world of frost and bite?

About you I don't care little sparrow
In my warm and happy home
As I snuggle up in bed
With tasty dreams ready to roam.

But angry little sparrow
Goes off and buys a gun
And comes back to shoot me dead
Just before a dream got the chance to run.

Now contented little sparrow
Kicks me to the floor,
Then dives into my bed
To sleep in warmth forevermore.

MOOD FOR A NUDE

There she turns into a portrait
For the fingers of perverted art,
And while her breasts are sleeping
She lets out a cunning fart.

The room is full of stink
And the art students fall away,
Just as she breathes her last
Then falls down as dead as night in day.

The cleaner comes and sweeps her up
Into the sack of forget,
Where history screams for vengeance
As we live on our lives in blind regret.

THE CRAZY CAT CHASE

There is a cat on the mat
That came up here from Hell
To scratch and bite
Throughout the night
And cast me 'neath her spell!
So me without a shred of doubt
Will be her poke and bell
With beard unweird
All strange and beered
I'll kiss her bum as well!

A GHOST OF LOVE

Hopes! Flying away.
People never cared.

Houses fat with ghosts:
Empty failures fill the
Graveyard heart of memory.

And there she stands
In portrait not in flesh.
She stole away for better
Just like all of the rest.

Now lonely in silence
I dwell in my dreams:
I am safe,
I am cured;
Where in real life
I've never been.

Now Time comes to kiss me
And say "Goodbye!"
As I lay down to die
And not one tear will I cry.
A
Sea of cobwebs trails away with grace.

BURN WITCH!

Words like car wheels
Race and scream away
Just like the luckless witch
That those fools burnt up
In darkness day.

Sadness creeps upon me
As if a new skin
Has come my way,
But bringing nothing new
To grow a smile over
And play!

Play!
That word is foreign.
Play!
That word does not belong
Here in my armour
That is so full of weakness
And never enough the
Strong.

Words to take
Or throw away
Like the kindness
We seldom give.
Am I now that endless fire
To which those fools
Condemned that witch?!

SHIT ME!

I shit you, baby,
You shit me too!
And all our love
Drips like dirt
Out of view.
The sky is easy,
The clouds are blue;
Just like your temper
When I put the touch on you.
I ran for justice
High above the sky,
But the Old Man was sleeping
Like a pig in a sty.
So back I came
All rusting true;
The end of romance -
The end of me and you.

Violins, please!
More BEER!

POEM FOR NO ONE

Poem for no one -
There's nothing to say!
All the sparrows sang tears
For the world today.

Shall I dig up the graveyard
And rewrite man?-
Much better than God did
With His diabolical plan!

No I'll sit empty
Like the future on high,
And just wait for the day
When I can finally die.

Cry!
Why bother?
Nobody gives a damn!

DEATH OF THE GOOD-TIME GIRL

Purelove put her finger in my face.
I did not like it and
Bit her cheese sandwich in half.
The eggs of her eyes
Growled in anger,
As the worm on her head
Danced a jig,
Then dived upon me
To lick, to kiss,
To blow away the clouds of joy
That stood there still and stupid
To their impending fate of death!
I cried out!
I felt pain – I screamed!
And then the dragon began!

Purelove, hands of clean,
Found herself trapped inside
A deliberately locked suitcase!
Her body bones, all squashed up,
Fell out of favour with cool
And sobbed out in agony.
I laughed.
I contentedly hummed!
And, yes, I even grinned!
Such evil!
Madness became me!

READY TO BEGIN

Today I have finished school.
Tonight I shall throw out
Of my mind
All of the blatant lies
That they taught me at school.
Life is for living.
May the death bed of fire
Hold the teacher
Fast for ETERNITY.
To lie is to sin.
And to sin is to die.

ARE WE REAL?

A double kiss for my woman for
She has given me hope,
Helped me cope
In these hard and bitter days
Where the fool is king
And the damned hold sway.

The war begins!
We got married today.

JOSHUA'S BALLOON

Joshua Croon
Lives in a balloon
And he floats around the world.
See him there;
A big blue blob
Up in the air,
And looking down
He sees all the filth below:
Drug dealer steals another life
In the rain, sun and snow.

So high, so free,
Up there where it's cool to be
With no worries, no pain,
While the rest of the world
Goes slowly down the drain.

Joshua Croon
Up in his balloon
Bakes pan cakes everyday
In the sun
With a bird and drum
He wastes his life away.
And looking down
He sees the ghosts below:
People like you and me
With no place good to go.

So high, so free,
Up there is the place to be
With no lover, no pain,
But that can never be you and me.

Joshua Croon
High in his balloon
Got shot down yesterday
By a
Government plan
And they'll do what they can
To make you live their way.
And looking down
All you'll see is more and more of the same:
Everybody in a line
To be brainwashed every hour to play their
Demon game.

So high, so free,
Joshua Croon's back up in the sky,
But this time as a spirit
Because to do it he had to die.

WHO THE HELL?!

Joe Udder: “I'm not writing a love poem for you,
You're horrible!
I can never do anything right!
I wear all the wrong clothes!
I smell!
I never shave!
I eat the wrong food!
I drink far too much beer
And smoke too many cigarettes!
And, on top of that,
I'm crap in bed!
How dare you?!
You're a right bitch!
Go to hell, you bastard!
Get your stuff and get out!
Go and ruin some other fool's life -
You're not wrecking mine anymore!
You even tried to drive my friends
Away from me!
You evil bitch!”

Sarah Blumb: “Wwwaaarrrgggghhhhh!”

Joe Udder: “Don't turn the crocodile tears on with me,
You cow!
It won't work!
Go and Moo away in a field somewhere!
Big fat ass on ya!
Go on a diet!

Squelching around everywhere!
Who do you think you are,
Mister Blob?

But I love you!
Yes, in some bizarre way!
For you light the candles
That put light into my day.

Yes, I love you.
You are so petite.
You're all sugar and spice,
And everything so sweet – oow!"

Sarah Blumb: "Get yer dick out! I need a hard shag after that, you wanker!"

HUNGRY LOVE

I fancied that woman;
Her buttocks were profound,
And with my hands upon them
True happiness could be found!
We kissed and we cuddled
By the dance of the moon
And, weaving after midnight,
She turned into a werewolf
And ate me without fork and spoon!

LONELINESS

I would like to talk to you
Everyday.
I would like to see you.
Please don't go away.

Here I am waiting
Until the sun turns into the moon.
Loneliness is killing me - oh!
Will I burn out to die so soon?

So now if I talk to you
Will you listen?

I 'd like to say:
“Why do you cry everyday?”

There's always a tear
In your eye.

I'd like to make you smile.

But she just walked away
Like a ghost!

There she is again
Standing by the swimming pool;
The water laughing like
Ripples in the wind.

Tears on her face falling
All the time!
And
Here I am
On my own
Everyday.
I look in the mirror
And I find that
She is me!

The tears of loneliness are
Drowning me,
And the swimming pool laughs!
Those ripples will kill me,
Kill me,
Kill ....!

THEM!

They took the old man to the cellar
And tied him to a chair.
They stole his face
And created chaos
Everywhere.
Now they run the country,
Now they rule our lives,
Now they take everything.

The old man broke free
And painted a new face to wear.
He shouted out the warning,
But nobody would believe him;
They laughed and mocked him
Everywhere.
So he ran away to a mountain
Where he saw an alien spaceship
And, jumping into it,
He flicked a big V at us,
Then flew off far away!

And we, like fools, remain
To endure.

THE PICTURE

Yes!
Silly!
Yes!
Silly me!
A chance, a chance!
Silly me,
I thought you had the eye,
But my sun got crossed
By a cloud!
So it's “No!”
And goodbye.

Still you ain't no picture anyway.
So why should I care?
But you kidnapped my soul,
And you carry on totally unaware.

Help me, help me!
I do not want to remain here!
These rooms are so cold and dark;
No love could ever hope to grow here.

But now the cloud has gone away,
And you've got me with a new look!
I'm transforming from a slum house
Into a castle with a rook!
Hey now we're moving,
And the way is clear,

So after all I've found a woman – yes!
Now I'm really here!

You are the picture
In a golden frame,
And I'm the prince of clowns
Who just hooked a ride
On your train.

MUCKY LOVE

The muck of her life
Pours out of her huge bum
Every night when we transport into bed.
Damn!
She farts so loud and hard-boiled
That it frightens away the ghosts
That used to congregate in the attic -
Marvellous!
Who would think that such
A dainty little woman
Could fill the world with such
An evil stink!
Never the less, or more,
I always partake of her fountain
And then fill her with
Goo!

THE NEVER GIRL

Great fascinating talk as
The eyes of the world unite,
And the blind Pink brothers
Touched Ember's heart in the fall.

Lately Robert opened a shop,
Wile red crystal fingers
Come upon the sleeping,
And Ember turns to stone!

Incredible strange town
All green in winter snow,
And there Ember leaves her prince
To play jazz with the hawk.

The doctor with a potion
Hunts Ember down,
But his task for the prince
Drives Ember out of town.
Far away.
Gone, gone.
Let emptiness hold sway.

PEOPLE IN FLAME

Her parents in the Hunting Hen
Did not like him:
“Marry him and you'll get nothing from me!”
Her father growled.
Sara was a-flixed!
Cried did the love spirit inside her.
“You'll find someone better, lass,”
Mother brushed in with firm
Washing hands.
Sara became grim,
Picked up a knife and left the pub.
Down street into street
Without a wave or laugh there to greet
Or meet,
Then into her beloved's flat with
Her cherished key.
Ian, her lover, was in
With happy kisses waiting,
But soon the knife
Was in him!
Dead he fell.
“If I can't have him,” Sara cried.
“Then no one will.”
She then stuffed her head in the oven
And cooked herself for dinner.

SEX MOMENT

Her big breasts like toys
Played with my fingers,
While the bed ate both
Our bodies in a frantic surge
Of love.
"In me, in me!" she screamed
With swords dancing in her eyes.
"The very me!" I roared,
As Planet Venus
Went streaking by.

THE LIFELESS LIGHT

If all we are
Is what you said,
Then it would have been better
If we'd both been born dead.
It doesn't matter;
We never tried,
Our time was burnt out
Long before you arrived.
So don't ask me,
And don't expect
One last smile
That I know I will regret.

Now the ghost goodbye.
Now the empty space.
Now the angry silence
That hangs
Lost in chains in my face.
And so all we had
Was never real,
And now in the end the lifeless light
Is all that we can feel.

OLD CARPETS

Old carpets in the shop window -
Special price today!:
Buy one get one free -
The Hard Sale all the way!

Got to move these carpets.
Got to get them out.
Got to make some money.
Got to sell without a doubt.

Faded carpets in the shop window
Are now turning green with age!
Got to get them out!
Got some new one's coming in!
Turn another page.

Someone came in today,
Looked at the carpets,
Then went away.
Now he's come back with a shotgun
To, he says, blow me away!

Shot dead for selling old carpets -
Is nothing sacred anymore?
Now the old carpets will never sell -
So sad!
Still, here in death,
I don't carpet care at all.

MAN DAY

Grum day!
Not a woman in the world for me.
At least I'm not dating that
Slag anymore.
She slept around behind my back.
I heard she got AIDS – ha!
Now to be clean again
There's no way back for her.
So much for your dolls
And your nursery rhymes.
You're just filth from head to foot!

Grim Day!
The rain is making my house fall down,
And I've got nowhere else to go!
I've got no friends anywhere.
My life is mine alone.
But I feel nearly happy.
At least I am free now
To search, to find
The real man
Living inside of me.

"Hello me!"

The mad silence!
This is like talking to God!

ANOTHER WAY

Saw the enemy coming on a hazy cloud
Phased behind a nuclear shroud.
Another war,
Another day,
How can we expect to prosper in this way?

Empty skull burning in the sand
And Man stood naked across the land.
Another bomb,
Another way,
To find the answer one day.

A sea of words filled with blood and hate
As now we see the hell of all human fate.
Another war,
Another day,
And you'll never see Truth
Walk down this way.

THE FIELDS OF NASHA

And so,
Without a ghost to my name,
I came,
Without pistol or tank,
To see,
I never paint pictures at midnight,
Her face,
That womb is full of fish!
Upon the sea,
But CDs skip sometimes,
With another man,
He stole the bank before the money was made,
She ran away!
I will give Nasha my beef steaks daily,
So I killed,
Nasha is getting fat,
Her here today,
In the flat yard behind our house,
And let no man laugh;
In time I'll need a bath
Full of soap and Nasha to know
As now off to jail I go.

Nasha has moved back home with her mother,
While they put,
Her hands grow bigger every evening,
The sun to bed and me in a cell,
But love will speak out,

With a hard man,
My kiss will bring my Nasha back,
Sent from hell,
I send flowers all the time,
But I would,
I post her boxes of chocolates too!
Not let him,
I feel her blush at my romantic way,
Have his way,
As he tried to kiss me everyday,
Nasha sleeps in a big cold bed,
Then one night
Into a werewolf I did turn,
But Nasha never saw me,
And so to my feverish lips
His flesh did learn.

I ate him!

Next,
While Nasha slept on for one hundred years,
And rotted away into a big dead fish,
I escaped my way out of the cell by
Eating through a wall – yum!
They buried Nasha without guilt or shame,
Concrete soup for one and all,
Then up a pipe
And onto the prison roof
Where Nasha wasn't waiting,
But God was -
He had His birth certificate with Him

To prove who He was!
Meanwhile,
Without breaking up graves or words,
I gave God the thumbs up,
Then ran away and fell off the roof
And here now I lie smashed and dying
On the firm-breasted ground.

I awake,
The moon is asleep,
And here in Hell I now stand
With Nasha,
My Venus in Furs,
Close to hand
With
Beer and sex,
Drugs and perversions to play,
As I transform into a demon
To re-emerge on Planet Earth
And come wicked down your way – ha, ha!
Beware!
I'll be coming soon
To fill your world with doom and gloom.
But first let me enjoy the pleasures
That are,
Without soldier or tramp,
The fields of Nasha!

CHOMPER'S BIT

I'm a bit,
I shovel shit,
And the wife can't fry
Sausages without
Setting fire to our love life.

Big bed
Smells a bit,
But we get it done.
Sleeping is for people
Who live in wardrobes.
Take note:
Fuck! Fuck! Fuck!

Each other,
Without a part,
We bake the onion
And rejoice
In the heart.

Good life.
For a bit.
Old is bad;
Now getting slow
And unfit.

Soon to die........
Goodbye.

JOSEPH BINDER

Joseph Binder
In the sky;
A little head
Floating by.
He had it all,
But threw it all away
In the mad chase of love
That destroyed his day.

Joseph Binder
Wound up dead;
A silver bullet
In his head.
She said: "No!"
He cried away
To end his life
This very sad day.

The house is empty,
The dream is gone,
But the seed is planted
To again carry on.......!

SPACES

In spaces I exist
To be one day washed away.
All of my smudge on life
Comes to
Nothing
As a new dog barks
Today.

RELIGIOUS DAYS

The day has turned into a wardrobe
With stuffed shirts everywhere
And dark silent places
Lurking like demons in the background;
Near the streets where the poor people
Fall over themselves to make money
Any which way beyond and before
The question:
Would God be agreeable to this kind
Of behaviour?
We may never know.
The slaughter of good goes on....!

THE ABSENT CADDIE

On Boulder's Grove
The hole awaits supreme,
And after lots of swearing
The golfer hits the green.
But his eyes are burning
And his soul is dead;
He's just blamed and killed his caddie
Back there behind the caretaker's shed.

Now the police are coming
As the final hole begins to smell,
And with handcuffs dangling
They'll swing him off to the nearest prison
Cell.

OPIUM FILL

Go on then,
Go on then,
My world is full of everything.
I take,
I take,
I never give.

See your house,
See your house,
It was always meant for me.
I'll take away,
Leave you naked
Howling in the scream!

Never born,
Never born,
A heart never grew in me.
Now I see you take revenge,
And slaughtered I deserve to be.

Big blue future sky,
Big blue future sky,
Awakes for you;
While hard steel and concrete
Prison walls
Now open wide to
Eat and whip me
Through and through.
Boo-hoo!

FANTASTIC TEARS!

The face of a pea
Appeared at the window
And looked in on me.
The pea then turned
Into a carrot
And flew away.
It then began to rain,
And the humble day ahead
Began to cry....!

EMPTY CHRISTMAS CARD

Empty Christmas Card from June;
It swings without snowdrops
Below the moon:
Below the clouds,
Below the dawn,
Upon the mantelpiece
Where the dust lies forlorn.
So it's goodbye to Christmas,
No cheer for me today;
I just look out the frosty window
And watch the snowman melt
Away....!

GRAVE MEDALS

Old man on crumbly legs
Crawling to the grave;
Where weeds like enemies wait to greet him,
And steal all of the victory that his youth gave:
To the weak,
To the lost,
To the world
At such a senseless cost.

Old man in his grave
Hears the last salute;
So they never forgot him!
Now they'll have to seed another brute.

THE POO-POO YEARS

Nappy poo-poo
On the line
Washed and cleaned
Doing fine.
Baby laughing
Throughout the day
With another poo-poo
On the way!

Other books by J. J. Williams

Novels:

Nonsense In Australia
Vak's War
Peacock Island
A Demon A Day
The Frightened Ghost

Poetry:

Boat
Lady On A G String
The Seven Fields Of Summer
Silly Hairy Legs
Weird Words
Wintle's Way
Who Stole The Poem At The Top Of The World?
The Wicked Fingers Of Delight
Yellow Windows
The Feathers Of Eden
Weeping For The Chain-Strap Of Freedom
When My Elephants Get Too Heavy
The Last Saxophone Of Summer
Parker Face
Empty Art
The Planet Has Grown Wings To Fly Away From You
Strangely Words
Living Without Boats
Cradle Fish

My Feet Have Set Me On Fire!
The Naked Womb
The Swing Dance Days Of Mary Loo!
The Worms Have Taken The Living
Mrs Shamshank's Lost Boiled Egg
Dove Kiss, my beauty
Jungle Feet Blue
The House Of Moncure'
Elder Glide
Wonder Wail
Calamity Brain
He Strummed His Guitar

www.ingramcontent.com/pod-product-compliance
Lightning Source LLC
LaVergne TN
LVHW050338160826
845677LV00014B/3675
9798418735225